Brewster
the
Rain-Makin'
Rooster

Published in the United States of America
By Eakin Press
A Division of Sunbelt Media, Inc.
P.O. Box 90159
Austin, TX 78709
email: eakinpub@sig.net
Visit us on the web at
www.eakinpress.com

1-57168-357-7

Library of Congress Cataloging-in-Publication Data

Ross, Tim, 1954-
     Brewster the rain makin' rooster / written by Tim Ross;
illustrated by Scott Ross.
     p.   cm.
     "A Professor Wigglestix book."
     Summary: Brewster, an intelligent rooster, successfully predicts the
weather, spelling out his forecast by scratching on the ground.
     ISBN 1-57168-332-1
     [1. Roosters Fiction. 2. Weather forecasting Fiction. 3. Stories in
rhyme.]   I. Ross, Scott, ill. II. Title.
     PZ8.3.R7434Br 1999
     [E]--dc21   99-36029
                                                                CIP

Brewster

the
Rain-Makin'
Rooster

A PROFESSOR WIGGLESTIX BOOK

Written by
Tim Ross

Illustrated by
Scott Ross

EAKIN PRESS ❦ Austin, Texas

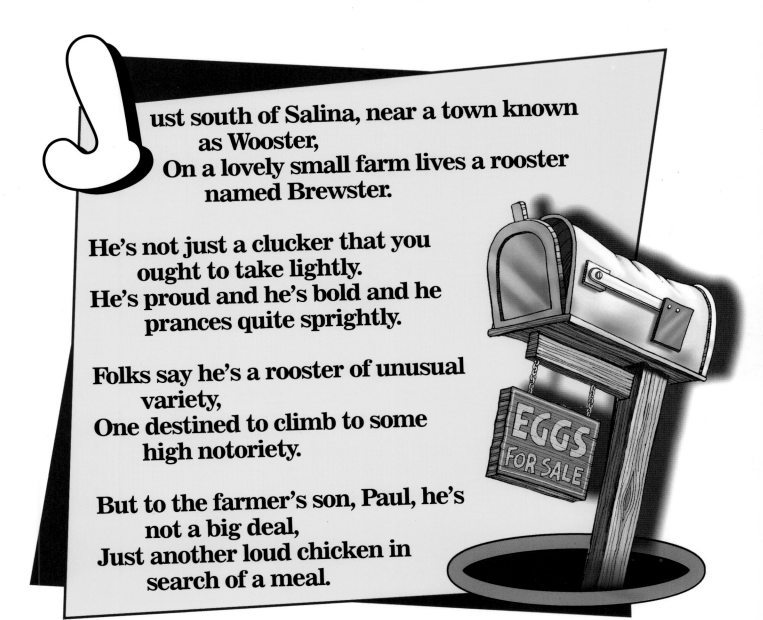

Just south of Salina, near a town known as Wooster,
On a lovely small farm lives a rooster named Brewster.

He's not just a clucker that you ought to take lightly.
He's proud and he's bold and he prances quite sprightly.

Folks say he's a rooster of unusual variety,
One destined to climb to some high notoriety.

But to the farmer's son, Paul, he's not a big deal,
Just another loud chicken in search of a meal.

Long about sunrise each day, give or take,
Out to ol' Brewster a trip does Paul
make.

It's one of his chores that he does twice a day.
Perhaps not his favorite, but he says, "It's
okay."

This day would be different, and quite a
surprise.
This one would really pop open Paul's eyes!

He crawled out of bed, though still half
asleep.
When he got to the birds he could hear 'em
all peep.

They were hungry, it seems, and just
couldn't wait,
For Paul to throw open that small
wooden gate.

Paul worked his way back
to the end of the coop.
Last, but not least, he threw
Brewster a scoop.

His fine-feathered friend schnarfed it right down.
No kernels of corn did he leave on the ground.

But still he kept pecking, that silly ol' bird.
When the dust had all settled, Paul noticed a word.

Brewster had scribbled the word "RAIN" in the dirt.
And as hot as it was, a quick squirt wouldn't hurt.

Paul was amazed and threw Brewster more corn.
Then another small wonder his rooster performed.

With a twitch and a twaddle, and then a small tweak,
The bird scratched the words "NEXT WEEK" with his beak!

Paul was in shock, and not a little bedazed.
At Brewster the Rooster he was truly
amazed!

If this clucker was right, the drought
would be broken,
But the source of this news could never
be spoken.

Who would believe him? Who could he tell?
Everyone knows that a chicken can't
spell.

"Paul," they would ask, "are you
feeling all right?
Brewster can't speak, and you know
he can't write!"

Paul kept to himself for the
rest of the day.
He told not a soul, not a word
did he say.

Weatherman Tim, on the TV that night,
Told of the drought, and its terrible plight.

He went on to say that no rain would be falling.
Yes, once again, Mom Nature was stalling.

Paul couldn't forget what he saw Brewster do,
And Weatherman Tim would want to know too.

He picked up the phone and gave it a dial.
"May I please speak to Tim?" he asked with a
    smile.

Weatherman Tim came right to the phone,
And the farmer's son, Paul, quickly drove his
    point home.

Paul told the story of Brewster's
    great feat,
And Weatherman Tim
    thought his story was
    neat.

"Paul, I must tell you," Tim
    said with all candor,
"I'd like to come out and take
    a small gander!"

The next day at noon, the news crew arrived,
To see if this story of Brewster survived!

Paul took 'em right to him—the rooster was real!
But Tim wasn't sure he'd perform for his meal.

Paul threw a few kernels of corn on the ground
And straight to the feast ol' Brewster did bound.

He gobbled 'em up, and still he kept pecking,
Was he writing the words that Paul was expecting?

"Yes, there it is!" Paul screamed with delight!
"I told you he could—I told you last night!"

"RAIN VERY SOON," it was plain as can be,
Scratched in the dirt for the news crew to see.

Tim's crew from the station stood there dumbfounded,
Confused, and amazed, and completely confounded!

Was what they had seen just a bunch of dumb luck,
Or was Brewster the Rooster one mighty smart cluck?

"Next week" came so quickly, the weather still hot.
The sun was still burning, and rain there was *not*!

The ponds were all dry, and so were the creeks,
You'd be dry too with no drink for eight weeks!

Tim's competition, those guys across town,
Were forecasting sun—they weren't backing down!

Said Weatherman Tim, "I've a decision to make.
What should I do? Which road should I take?"

Now, Weatherman Tim was a popular guy,
And if Brewster was right, his ratings would fly!

But forecasting rain when the computers say, "Sunny!"
Might ruin his name, and that's not too funny!

Just then the phone rang—it was Paul at the farm,
Yes, Brewster the Rooster had pulled the alarm!

"RAIN BY TOMORROW!" he had scratched in the dirt.
And Paul was convinced they'd get a big squirt.

im was excited, but Tim was still
   sensible.
   To make a mistake would be
   indefensible!

He thought long and hard, then thought once
   again.
Still he kept thinking until suddenly when . . .

"I'll do it! I'll do it!" screamed Weatherman
   Tim.
"I'm forecasting rain, though chances
   seem slim!"

So later that night, on the tube he did go,
To forecast some rain and let
   everyone know!

The phones rang a lot . . . they
   rang off the wall!
"Your weatherman's nuts!"
   they said when they called.

Much later that night, some storm
clouds were forming.
It appeared that ol' Brewster was
right with his warning.

Not long after that, the rain began falling,
And falling . . . and falling . . . and falling . . .
and falling.

The next day in the paper the headlines
were huge,
About Weatherman Tim, and his
stormy deluge!

He was the "talk of the town,"
and that's putting it lightly.
His weathercasts, now, the
whole town would watch
nightly.

WEATHERMAN TIM
SHOCKS EXPERTS!

For the next several months Tim's
forecasts were right.
He never missed once–not one single night!

When he called for some rain, the rain always
fell,
And the same was true for wind, snow, and
hail.

His ratings rose quickly to the top of the
heap.
But of Brewster the Rooster, there wasn't
a peep!

Tim was excited, but he knew the
whole story.
It was Brewster the Rooster who
deserved all the glory.

Tim would consult his maps, charts,
and science,
But on Brewster the Rooster
there was total reliance.

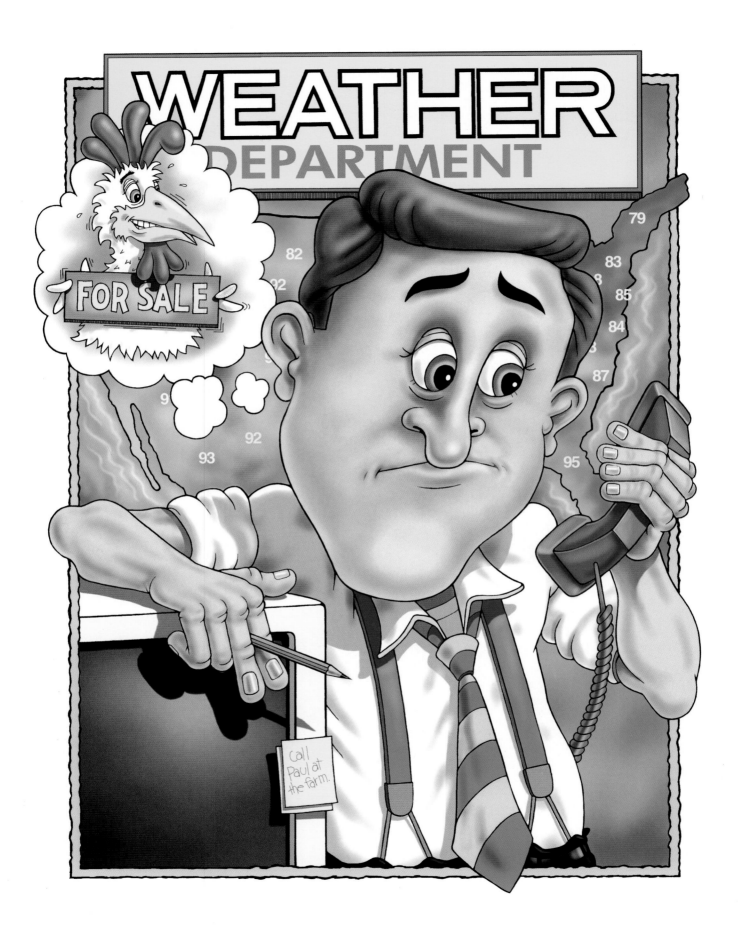

So imagine Tim's shock when Paul shared the words
That his father, the farmer, was selling his birds!

"Did I hear you right? He'll be selling his birds?"
To Weatherman Tim, these were startling words!

Tim asked again, "Are you sure this is true?
What can be done? What can I do?"

The buyer had spoken, and soon they'd be gone.
But Tim raised his voice, "Yuh gotta hold on!"

"Give me some time, I'll think this thing through,
I've gotta decide what it is I can do!"

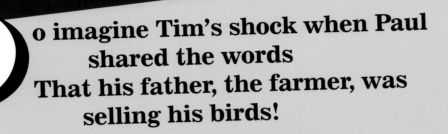

e worried that day, and the next day
as well.
He wondered aloud when the
chickens might sell.

Weatherman Tim 'bout drove himself nuts.
He needed that rooster, no ifs, ands, or buts!

Though Tim knew nothing of chickens or
farming,
The thought of this loss was very
alarming.

He got on the phone and
talked to Paul's dad,
He wanted those chickens,
he wanted 'em bad!

BREWSTER

Weatherman Tim and Paul's father,
    the farmer,
    Got together to talk, and ol' Tim
    was a charmer.

The farmer knew nothing of Brewster's
    great talent,
So Tim's "chicken pitch" seemed rather
    gallant.

He sold Tim the chickens, the rooster
    included.
   "Now Brewster is mine!" Tim shouted and
    hooted.

It had been a close call, there
    was no doubt about that.
But Brewster was Tim's, so
    he'd stay where he's at.

For Brewster the Rooster, the red
carpets rolled out.
That this clucker was special, could
there be any doubt?

The station constructed a most beautiful
facility
For their chicken of choice . . . this bird of
nobility.

No chicken had lived in a coop quite so
beautiful
But not many roosters had been
so darn dutiful!

Paul kept the BIG secret, not
a soul did he tell.
And his rooster was happy, so
that's just as well.

And Weatherman Tim flashed a
bright TV grin,
'Cause his forecasts were
right—again and again!

WEATHER STUFF

COMPUTERS

There are a lot of computers in Mr. Tim's weather center. Each one does a different job. The most important computers help him to analyze stuff like the wind, temperatures, humidity, rain, and snow. He wouldn't be able to forecast the weather without them. And sometimes the forecasts are wrong even with the help of all of his fancy computers. Oooooops!!!

But the work doesn't stop there! Weatherman Tim has to find a way to get that information to you. For that he uses a graphics computer. This computer makes all of the maps and neat pictures you see on his weathercasts. His daughter thinks he colors pictures for a living. His fans think he has an easy job because they see him work on TV for only three minutes a day. But it takes a lot of work to get all of those maps and weathercasts on TV. He's a very dedicated guy!

Weatherman Tim

WORLDWIDE WEATHER RECORDS

Lowest Temp	Highest Temp
-129 °	*136 °*
July 21, 1983	September 13, 1922
Vostok, Antarctica	El Aziza, Libya (Africa)

Most Rainfall	Most Rainfall
Most In One Year	*Most In One Hour*
905"	*12"*
1861	June 22, 1947
Cherapunji, India	Holt, MO

Most Snowfall	Highest Wind Gust
* Most In One Season	*5 Minutes Duration
1122"	*231 mph*
July 21, 1983	April 12, 1934
Mt. Rainier, WA	Mt. Washington, NH

SATELLITES

Have you ever seen a tiny little dot of light moving slowly across the night sky? You probably saw a high-flying man-made satellite launched into space from Earth. Some of these satellites are designed for weather forecasting. They fly almost 23,000 miles above the Earth. The first weather satellite was named TIROS I. It was launched into space in 1961. The newest satellites are called GOES 8 and 9 and cost almost $2 billion each. Will they ever fall from the sky? No . . . they're glued up there! Seriously, you're safe . . . they're up there to stay!

AMS "SEAL OF APPROVAL"

The Television *Seal of Approval* of the American Meteorological Society is very special. Only the best meteorologists are permitted to display the seal. Only 900 TV meteorologists worldwide are allowed to display it.

RADAR

Try spelling RADAR backwards! Pretty neat, huh? That's exactly what radar does. A very powerful but harmless electronic signal is sent into the sky from the radar. When that signal hits the rain, hail, or snow the signal bounces back to the radar. The computer attached to the radar is able to figure out how much rain or snow is falling and where the rain or snow is located. Sometimes the radar can make a mistake. It might indicate rain when, in fact, it is detecting a flock of birds or a dust storm. Radar is a very complicated electronic tool. It takes about two years of training to learn how to properly use radar. It's Weatherman Tim's favorite tool. He thinks RADAR is waaaaayyy cool!

Is That A Radar Car?

And did you know that police officers use radar too? It's true! They are very small radar units which are used to catch people who are driving too fast. Better slow down . . . or you might get a ticket!